A Little Owl Book  Holt, Rinehart & Winston, Inc., New York

Old Mother Goose

With drawings by Frederick Richardson

Adapted by Frank Haines

Copyright © 1963 by Holt, Rinehart and Winston, Inc.
Library of Congress Catalog Card Number 63-12406
Printed in the United States of America
4-9770-1913

OLD KING COLE

OLD King Cole
    Was a merry old soul,
And a merry old soul was he;
    And he called for his pipe,
    And he called for his glass,
And he called for his fiddlers three!

Every fiddler he had a fine fiddle,
    And a very fine fiddle had he;
Twee-tweedle-dee, tweedle-dee, went the fiddlers.
Oh, there's none so rare as can compare
    With King Cole and his fiddlers three!

ROBIN AND RICHARD

ROBIN and Richard were two pretty men,
    They lay in bed till the clock struck ten;
Then up starts Robin and looks at the sky,
"Oh, brother Richard, the sun's very high!
You go before with the bottle and bag,
And I'll come after on jolly Jack Nag."

HICKETY, PICKETY

HICKETY, pickety, my
    black hen,
She lays eggs for gentlemen;
Gentlemen come every day
To see what my black hen
    doth lay.

THERE WERE TWO CATS OF KILKENNY

THERE were two cats of Kilkenny,
  Each thought there was one cat too
    many,
So they fought and they fit,
And they scratched and they bit,
Till, excepting their nails
And the tips of their tails,
Instead of two cats there weren't any.

SEE A PIN AND PICK IT UP

SEE a pin and pick it
  up,
All the day you'll have
  good luck.
See a pin and let it lay,
Bad luck you'll have all
  the day.

EVENING RED

EVENING red and morning grey
  Sends the traveler on his way;
Evening grey and morning red
Brings down rain upon his head.

THIS LITTLE PIG WENT TO MARKET

THIS little pig went to market;
　　This little pig stayed at home;
This little pig had roast beef;
This little pig had none;
This little pig cried, "Wee, wee, wee!"
　　All the way home.

LITTLE TOM TUCKER

LITTLE TOM TUCKER
  Sings for his supper:
What shall he eat?
  White bread and butter.
How shall he cut it
  Without e'er a knife?
How can he marry
  Without e'er a wife?

TOM, TOM, THE PIPER'S SON

TOM, Tom, the piper's son,
  Stole a pig, and away he run.
The pig was eat, and Tom was beat,
And Tom went crying down the street.

  Tom, Tom, was a piper's son,
  He learned to play when he was young;
  But the only tune that he could play,
  Was "Over the hills and far away."

Tom with his pipe made such a noise,
That he pleased both the girls and boys;
They'd dance and skip while he did play,
"Over the hills and far away."

Tom with his pipe did play with such skill,
That those who heard him could never keep still;
As soon as he played they began for to dance;
Even pigs on their hind legs would after him
   prance.

OLD MOTHER HUBBARD

OLD Mother Hubbard went to the cupboard,
   To get her poor Dog a bone;
But when she came there, the cupboard was bare,
   And so the poor Dog had none.

She went to the baker's
   To buy him some bread,
But when she came back,
   The poor Dog was dead.

She went to the joiner's
   To buy him a coffin,
But when she came back,
   The poor Dog was laughing.

She took a clean dish
   To get him some tripe,
But when she came back,
   He was smoking a pipe.

She went to the hatter's
   To buy him a hat,
But when she came back
   He was feeding the cat.

She went to the barber's
   To buy him a wig,
But when she came back,
   He was dancing a jig.

She went to the seamstress
To buy him some linen,
But when she came back,
The Dog was a-spinning.

She went to the hosier's
To buy him some hose,
But when she came back,
He was dressed in his
clothes.

The Dame made a curtesy,
The Dog made a bow;
The Dame said, "Your servant,"
The Dog said, "Bow wow."

This wonderful Dog
Was Dame Hubbard's delight;
He could sing, he could dance,
He could read, he could
write.

She gave him rich dainties whenever he fed,
And erected a monument when he was dead.

I HAD A LITTLE PONY

I HAD a little pony;
  They called him Dapple-grey.
I lent him to a lady,
  To ride a mile away.
She whipped him, she lashed him,
  She rode him through the mire,
I would not lend my pony now,
  For all the lady's hire.

LADYBIRD, LADYBIRD

LADYBIRD, Ladybird,
  Fly away home,
Your house is on fire,
Your children will burn.

THERE WAS AN OLD WOMAN

THERE was an old woman tossed up in a
basket,
Seventeen times as high as the moon;
And where she was going, I couldn't but ask it,
For in her hand she carried a broom.

"Old woman, old woman, old woman," said I,
"O whither, O whither, O whither so high?"
"To sweep the cobwebs off the sky!"
"Shall I go with you?" "Aye, by and by."

BAT, BAT, COME UNDER MY HAT

BAT, bat, come under my hat,
And I'll give you a slice of bacon,
And when I bake I'll give you a cake,
If I am not mistaken.

SEE, SEE

See, see. What shall I see?
A horse's head where his tail should be.

PIT, PAT, WELL-A-DAY!

PIT, pat, well-a-day!
Little Robin flew away;
Where can little Robin be?
Up in yonder cherry tree.

ONE TWO, BUCKLE MY SHOE

One, two, buckle my shoe;

Three, four, shut the door;

Five, six, pick up sticks;

Seven, eight, lay them straight;

Nine, ten, a good fat hen;

Eleven, twelve, dig and delve;

Thirteen, fourteen, maids a-courting;

Fifteen, sixteen, maids in the kitchen;

Seventeen, eighteen, maids a-waiting;

Nineteen, twenty, my plate's empty.

SING A SONG OF SIXPENCE

SING a song of sixpence, a pocket full of rye;
  Four and twenty blackbirds, baked in a pie;
When the pie was opened, the birds began to
    sing,
Was not that a dainty dish to set before
    the King?

The King was in his counting house, counting out
    his money;
The Queen was in the parlor, eating bread
    and honey;
The maid was in the garden, hanging out the
    clothes;
Down came a blackbird, and snapped off
    her nose.

THERE WAS AN OLD CROW

THERE was an old crow
    Sat upon a clod.
There's an end of my song,
    That's very odd.

TO MARKET, TO MARKET

TO market, to market, to
    buy a fat pig,
Home again, home again,
    jiggety jig.
To market, to market,
    to buy a fat hog,
      Home again, home again,
      jiggety jog.

SEE-SAW, SACRADOWN

SEE-SAW, sacradown,
    Which is the way to London town?
One foot up and the other foot down,
And that is the way to London town.

BARBER, BARBER, SHAVE A PIG

BARBER, barber, shave a pig.
   How many hairs will make a wig?
Four and twenty; that's enough.
Give the barber a pinch of snuff.

LITTLE NANNY ETTICOAT

LITTLE Nanny Etticoat,
   In a white petticoat
And a red nose;
The longer she stands,
The shorter she grows.

GOOD KING ARTHUR

WHEN good King Arthur ruled this land,
　　He was a goodly King;
He bought three pecks of barley meal,
　　To make a bag-pudding.

A bag-pudding the King did
　make,
And stuffed it well
　with plums,
And in it put great lumps of
　fat,
As big as my two
　thumbs.

The King and Queen did eat thereof,
　　And noblemen beside;
And what they could not eat that night,
　　The Queen next morning fried.

CRY,
BABY,
CRY

CRY, Baby, cry,
　　Put your finger in your eye,
And tell your mother it wasn't I.

DICKERY, DICKERY, DOCK

DICKERY, dickery, dock!
    The mouse ran up the clock;
The clock struck one, and down he
    ran;
Dickery, dickery, dock!

MOLLY, MY SISTER, AND I FELL OUT

MOLLY, my sister, and I fell out,
      And what do you think it was about?
She loved coffee, and I loved tea,
And that was the reason we couldn't agree.

LITTLE GIRL

LITTLE girl, little girl, where
    have you been?
Gathering roses to give to the Queen.
Little girl, little girl, what gave she
    you?
She gave me a diamond as big as
    my shoe.

OLD MOTHER GOOSE

OLD Mother Goose, when
  She wanted to wander,
Would ride through the air
  On a very fine gander.

Mother Goose had a house,
  'Twas built in a wood,
Where an owl at the door
  For sentinel stood.

She had a son Jack,
  A plain-looking lad,
He was not very good,
  Nor yet very bad.

She sent him to market,
  A live goose he bought.
"Here, mother," says he,
  "It will not go for nought."

Jack's goose and her gander
  Soon grew very fond,
They'd both eat together,
  And swim in one pond.

Jack found one fine morning,
  As I have been told,
His goose had laid him
  An egg of pure gold.

Jack ran to his mother,
  The news for to tell,
She called him a good boy
  And said it was well.